Edward Wellmore

The soul's departure and other poems

Edward Wellmore

The soul's departure and other poems

ISBN/EAN: 9783744722704

Printed in Europe, USA, Canada, Australia, Japan

Cover: Foto ©Andreas Hilbeck / pixelio.de

More available books at **www.hansebooks.com**

THE CAMEO SERIES

The Soul's
Departure
and Other
Poems

Publisher's Note

THE Cameo Series, *commenced in
1889, was designed for the bring-
ing together, as opportunity offered,
of Volumes of Poetry of an original
quality. This programme was carried
out, in a modest way, by the inclusion
in the Series, among other volumes, of
William Watson's* Wordsworth Grave,
Amy Levy's London Plane Tree *and*
A Minor Poet, *and translations of
Ibsen's* Lady from the Sea *and* Brand,
and of Echegaray's The Son of Don
Juan *and* Mariana.

*The publisher in issuing Mr.
Willmore's* The Soul's Departure and
Other Poems, *begs to state that it is
the first of several new volumes planned,
which it is hoped may further justify
the original design of* The Cameo
Series.

The Soul's Departure

AND OTHER POEMS

by

EDWARD WILLMORE

CAMEO SERIES

T. Fisher Unwin Paternoster Sq.
London E.C. MDCCCXCVIII.

Contents

The Soul's Departure.

The Soul's Departure.

*" He shall return no
more to his house."*
JOB vii. 10.

WHEN the time came round
    That the Soul must leave the Body,
All the Man's kinsfolk
Stood round the bed
Where the miracle was to be
—The departure for the journey.
And the heavy eyelids
Gave faint recognition,
And the leaden hands
Caught at the coverlet :
Then the Soul stood out
Invisible beside the shed Body,
And shivered in the strange air.

Now when the mourners,
Performing the decent rites
To the still clay, had departed,
The trembling Ghost alone
Beheld its dead companion,
And lay close to it on the bed,.
And breathed in the nostrils,
And kissed the cheeks like a lover,
For well it knew
The inadequate use
It had made of the Body,
Now realising
Expression's postponement
Forever impossible ;
Whispering rapidly—
" Much have I marred thee,
Beautiful Body,
Gift of my Mother ;
Much have I starved thee
From fitting communion,
Till now thou seem'st
Heavy and strange to me.
O let me live in thee
Just for a day more—
The rest of this day—

Only an hour, then?
For I have twenty words
To say to my children,
And a score others
For my Wife Martha,
Words I have treasured
Fearing to utter them,
Thinking them too great."

To whom the Body
By faint intimations
(For each alone
Was understood by the other)—
" Much now I marvel
How half a hundred years
Then hast thou slighted me,
Keeping back from me
A portion of joy,
When I have yielded thee
Rights as a bride yields.
Was I inadequate?
From our Mother
I had my full limbs,
And it shames me to think
Their due is bereft.

Still is my tongue warm :
Was that inadequate ?
Did not my heart beat
Fully and sweetly,
Granting sufficiency ?
The ample tides of my blood,
Leaping for gladness,
Joyed in their channels.
Now it is late ;
I must rejoin—
Am now rejoining—
As thou in thy sphere,
The cycles of Being.
Alas !   Laggard lover,
Æons will lavish,
And not come again to this
In thy hand yesterday."
And the dead eyelids
Moistened and glinted,
And the very dead heart
Shivered,
Stopped.

Then the Soul
Trembled violently,

And the eight Doom-Angels
Entered the room,
Stark servants of God,
Bearing their heavy swords.

But when they looked on the bed
They perceived two corpses,
For the Soul like a corpse
Lay by the Body
In deadly affright ;
But by its fearful countenance
They knew it,
And questioned it straitly
In a moment of time
Concerning all its past life,
While it lay calm in dread,
As the Body in death.

Then they called the Soul to depart,
And out of the loved doorway it went,
Guarded by the Angels.
But when it reached the courtyard
(Now, loud-mouthed,
Howled the kennelled hounds,
Men's friends, cowed,

And cowering to rue—
Rough ones, to rue)
And beheld the window
At which so often
When homeward returning
It had seen the beloved ones,
The Ghost roused from its stupor
And tried to stay the guards
By its pitiful gesture.

But they advanced starkly.

Then it again besought them
With its pitiful gesture
(A wavering, thin cloud
Amidst those strong ones,
Destiny's executors,
Surcharged with direction,
Of path pre-appointed
Unto the World's end) :
" Let me one moment
Look in at the window
And see my Wife Martha
And the three Children again ;
Long is the way I needs must go,
And far will they be from me."

They replied, "We may not.
God would accuse us."
But still it besought
With its pitiful gesture :
"God will not accuse you
For one moment's delay.
And if He did not pity,
Would not you pity me ? "

Heaven's house-soldiers,
The guards of the high God,
Were moved at the Soul's words ;
They dropt their shining sword-points,
And the Man's Soul
Gazed in at the window-pane.

There the poor Wife Martha
Sat with the three Children
Near a glow of ashes,
And wept.
And the Soul wept too,
And moaned and shook the window,
And the youngest Child said joyfully,
" It is Father come home."

But the Mother started and said,
" It is the storm-gust."

So the Soul,
Struggling to speak,
Was borne on by the Angels.
Wearily it went the way,
Until on the right hand
Moved a dark ocean,
Moonless and starless ;
Forms flitted over it.
On the left were ice-mountains.
The wind's thong
Forever swung.
Dread was the noise of ice.

" Calligraphy."

" *Calligraphy*."

IN the Japanese pictures I saw what exceed-
    ingly pleased me :

Rivers ran over the roofs, clouds intercepted
    the soil ;

Men were inanities, maids were all of them
    pretty young simpletons,

And an elaborate care counted the hairs of the
    head ;

Dragons and demon-gangs leered at a shudder-
    ing welkin ;

Perfectly accurate fish — perfectly accurate
    scales.

Is not the sun of gold and is not the moon
    of crystal ?

Then we will have them so painted and stuck
    on the wall.

This is the law of Art, and now I can under-
    stand it :

Stray in a million ways, but always with
    constant mind.

Put in nothing too much, though you show
    feather-filaments ;

Nature knows her affairs, so you should know
    yours too.

Dead convention itself is better than nerveless
    daubing,

But the restraining grip on a powerful horse is
    the thing.

To the informing eye not hindered by bungling
    outlines,

Battle, advance, and retreat are even in splashes
    of rain.

Michel Angelo's David.

Michel Angelo's David.

IF from that forehead starry light should rise
   By some device—think you would that be
     Art ?
I almost think so.
Thou terrible ! That such a one as thou
Should tread the World's dust, let down thus to
   walk
Divine amongst confused and heathen men,
Much signifies. (Shout, wastes !) This is God's
   boy,

And ever the o'erarching Destiny
Moves over him, and ever murmuring moves
As the whole flood of the great upper air.
Com'st from that terrene brook that smooth'd
    the stone
And lookt young, but was immemorial ?
O rather from what high empyreal founts,
(Shout, deserts !) from what sources of the stars,
Outpouring empire, did this shepherd stray ?

Apollo, The Neatherd.

Apollo, The Neatherd.

I.

WITH care on his coat,
   And shame on his shoon,
Who knows such a note,
   And begets such a boon ?
Through the rents in his rags there is streaming
The sun, in its glinting and gleaming
   On the grass before noon.

II.

As he minded the cows
   A calling began
In the branches and boughs :
   " God Apollo ! " it ran.
Aloof the land-cliff, wan and hollow,
Repeated " Apollo ! Apollo ! "—
   But to man he was man.

III.

" O, lend me thy pipe
   For the rest of the day,
For the season is ripe,
   And the makers of hay "
(Said a youth with fair gesture advancing)
" Have need of a tune to their dancing ;
   Well as thou I can play."

IV.

So he lent him his flute,
   But he gave him also
To walk with dumb brute
   In a weft as of woe.
The god guileful flew back to his splendour,
And the man with a melody tender
   Is betrayed here below.

The Pedant.

The Pedant.

THE World is alive, it will never be still ;
The sea is a bit of the planet barefaced,
And the houses and streets that men build at
will
Are but a vesture momently placed,
Are but a dress
On the Earth-Mother's awful nakedness ;
And the rocks that are hurrying down in rain,
And the shimmering plain,

And the joys of trees and the struggles of seas
That cease and begin,
Are the Life, the Body, yea, the Skin.

    A man with a spade and mattock and book
Buried the World because it was dead,
And over it pattering prayers he said.
Black was his coat and his look.
He was sure that his thought was true,
That he held the key of the complex Whole,
And his theory of it was quite complete.
(Sad that it was as it was, and great rue,
As you saw by his face in the street,
Set with his iron imaginings
Superior-sad to the frame of things).
And firm was he
For the sexton's fee ;
And accordingly there was nought to do
But to bow with mind and soul
In the house of the man with the mattock, the
    book,
And the spade, and the key of the complex
    Whole.
And all were bowing, until a child,
Simple and mild,

Cried out: "O mother, there's a poor dead man
Who first dug his grave before he died !
O mother dear," (the little one cried)
" I love not the sight, and I never can."
Then the mother said, "Come, dear, come away,
For the beautiful World is alive to-day."

Lamps and Stars.

Lamps and Stars.

STILL causeless is Almighty Thought,
  Without beginning, without end ;
Each after each all things are wrought
  And to their purpose gladly tend.
The planets in their courses greet
The lamps that shine in this poor street.

And who shall slight one thing as small
  And praise another thing as great ?
Know ye the Thought of God is all,
  And blessèd they that on Him wait.
These stones Heaven's firmament are worth,
For they have borne a saint of Earth.

Ceaseless perfection, strong and bright,
   In lowly imperfection dwells,
And from the caverns of the night
   The everlasting Light upwells.
God left the sages to their fears
And whispers Truth in children's ears.

King of the Earth, grasp all below,
   And less than nothing now is thine.
King of the Earth, come down in woe,
   Stars on the manger-cradle shine,
Stars on the manger-cradle dwell ;
Thou Mary-mother, guard him well.

These flowers upon the pavement cast
   Are for thy feet.   Thy little son
Shall spread the ancient Word at last
   That on the high priest's forehead shone.
Horses at work the Word shall bear
Upon the bridles that they wear.

Queen Rose.

Queen Rose.

RED rose that loves the chosen breast
    With sweet-sure potency beguiling,
Joy-heavy to outshine the rest,
    So queenly bowing, queenly smiling.

(March came along with romp and whirl,
    But July is maturely human ;
The cowslip was a slender girl,
    But you, my dear, you are a woman).

As high you reign the flowers above,
   Your royal command I waited, seeking,
But, madam, you had told your love,
   And so you blushed instead of speaking.

The Noon Star.

The Noon Star.

THE noon sky reigned unfathomed, deeply-
    clear,
  Unmottled by the smallest argent cloud,
The bright black huts familiar stood and dear,
  And close beside them was a little crowd
Of fishermen and children. I drew near,
  Seeing them gaze above ; and then, not loud,
But with a cheerful reverence, one man said—
" Look up and see that wonder overhead."

We stood within the shadow. I suppose
   No day had ever shone with fairer light
Since with a boy's soul the first Day uprose,
   His girdle fastened by the matron Night.
The high sun gloried in his strength, as those
   Who fulfil both a task and a delight ;
And deep within that zenith, and afar
In that intensest azure, was one star.

Upon the bluish shingle a brown net
   Lay, and the sea with tender wooing prest
The uncoy beach as still as those who yet
   Are heaven-haven'd from the world's unrest.
"This star," the fisher said, "in light is set,
   That with long spells of calm we may be
     blest."
But to myself there came most joyously
The knowledge that it was a gift to me.

In the London Street.

c

In the London Street.

TWO angels at the dawn of day
   Stood watching in the London street
Beside a sleeper's curtained room.
   The flowers on the sill were meet.

The dull bricks caught the splendid glow,
   But I perceived that not alone
They glinted from the glance of day,
   But from the angels' swords that shone.

Reflecting shone, as fiery brands,
   Yet tempered adamant and bright ;
The rays, straight-darting, moved along,
   As eyelash-sparkles in the light.

I saw and knew God's messengers,
   White-vestured in the austere gray,
Strong and immovable they stood
   To light again our solar day.

And one was Truth.   Still at his word
   The common fact became sublime ;
He did unite in holiness
   The past unto the present time.

The other, Beauty, stood beside
   His fellow in divine control,
And was unto his shining peer
   As is a body to its soul.

The Midnight Cock.

The Midnight Cock.

DULL and sepulchral is the cope of midnight.
   Can a small shriller lift that leaden coffin ?
I am aweary, the proclaimer, weary,
            Weary but dauntless.

" Kokko " I'm called through all the land of
    Afric ;
Praised by Dan Chaucer, morning-man of
    England ;
Played I my part in the sublimest drama,
            Shamer of Peter.

Sleepy I crow, but still I crow though sleepy ;
In a few hours I shall possess my spirit,
Fire up the vast with one small spark of
    laughter,
           Call up the sun-ball !

Now o'er the world the sprites of evil ravin,
Weigh down my soul, but shall not choke my
　　　outcry,
" Kúckuru Rú," till all my far-off kinsmen
　　　　　　　　Answer " Kurúru."

What can a little bird or man achieve more?
Singing remembered love, I chase the darkness,
Thrusting aside obsceneness and oppression,
　　　　　　　　Prophet of Morning.

Swarms of small chirpers, little singers, poets,
All ye that copy, having nought within you,
Copy (you can't) my mystic tragi-comic
　　　　　　　　" Kúckuru—Rúru ! "

And if my tones should imitate the thunder,
Or by revulsion call up solemn feelings,
Don't be afraid.　My function is to govern
　　　　　　　　Six buxom houris.

Strength in Weakness.

Strength in Weakness.

OF the veils of the Immortals
  Ancient is the strange tradition,
As they come from Heaven's portals
  On some lone terrestrial mission.

Watch the sea's exulting horses—
  God is in the fountain's lavement.
Scan the storm's assailing forces—
  He, elusive, walks the pavement.

Excellent the sun advances,
  Yet is less than many another
Sun in midnight's pale expanses
  Wan as brow of nursing mother.

Not in priestly shams the Highest,
  (Ghastly sin of ghostly mumming)
They are still to God the nighest
  Who perceive His quiet coming.

The Crystal Window.

The Crystal Window.

THE words of the great Sultan. From the
   world
(I said in youth) I hold me hence unstained.
In antres, in an outpost of the soul
Kept by grave men, one noon I fell asleep.

Lo, in my visions on my bed, a pile
Whose cupolas, whose minarets, whose towers,
In myriad-fretted forms, as if the stone
Were plastic to the ocean-play of thought,
From Earth's deep matrix lifted to the clouds
That are unrolled beneath the throne of God.

Inwoven with the traceries all about,
I read strange characters : " This is the House
Of Human Thought."   This then, I said, is
    mine,
My treasure-palace and my wisdom-store ;
Mine, for the interscription indicates
The complement of my humanity.
No longer peaked in tents, I justly rise
To my own stature, and behold—Myself !
I entered, and as when one first inherits,
Strode the unpeopled halls ; when lo, in one
An ample window glowed with crystal tints
And bore the mystic saying : " Know Thyself."

    Know.   A high enterprise.   How might I
    know ?
I fell to study.   Thousand volumes there
Re-worded Man, as sultan, saint, recluse,
Or father of the poor, or sword of God
Upstaying mighty states ; or falling thence
To tire upon the wheel of five poor spokes ;
Or thence arisen, sprinkling the hot dust
Upon his head, giving the last small cruse,
Or breaking it upon the rock to Heaven.

Also I pondered elder secrets, told
By dealers at first-hand with mystic powers—
Great Solomon or Agur lowly-wise ;
Sabean wisdom of empyreal strengths,
The stark loins of Arcturus and his sons,
The Southern chambers, mighty Mazzaroth,
Sweet Pleiades, Orion terrible.
For years I eager read (the years of dreams)
And still mine eyes were fixed upon the books,
Admiring all the wisdom of mankind
For that it was my wisdom and myself.
So, like the sitting Memnon by old Nile,
I sat, adouble angle on a chair,
And watched the ages of the Universe.
At length I looked about, and saw it dark ;
A small lamp flickered.

              A great Presence stood,
An angel with a brow of regal wrath,
Silent.

    I bowed the head and begged his speech.
"O pardon.   Have I not fulfilled the law ?
Look, messenger, for thou canst see the heart,
Whom have I injured ?   From the firmament
Though thou hast come, I say it even to thee—

Within this heart is no ungenerous thought
To the oppressed of earth, or to God's poor."

Thus desperate, and for that royal blood
Fulfils my veins, I raised my soul 'gainst him,
Who from his height made answer :

" Get thee hence."
(One deep bell sounded whose residual tones
Pervaded all the palace). " Get thee hence.
The end of Man is action and not thought.
Did the Almighty make thy human soul
In jest ? How hast thou helped thy fellow-
      men ?
Where is thy work ? Innumerable forms
In darkness sit—thy brothers ; children, too,
And even these shall be thy judges."

Far
The world beyond the desert seemed to sigh.
The sleepy cock crew. Suddenly a chill
Of bitter air shook all my flesh. I glanced
Aloft—can Man forget ?—The window there
Was opened outwards, gone its blazoned words,
Gone the gay characters of " Know Thyself " :
Instead, behold, I saw through that embrasure—
The limitless abyss of starry night.

Dawn.

Dawn.

[Spitalfields.]

GRAY is the steeple austere in the still oper-
ations of morning,
Surely a house of hands, yet surely akin to
the cloud.
Far below are the tremulous trees that rustle
and glitter,
Down by the portico's gloom and the sleepy
awakening smoke.
Pigeon-companionships with a beautiful free
libration

Float, then flutter and fall, circle and swerve
    and sway.
Over the market-place (but everything hangs
    on an eyelash)
Strides the spirit that holds the leash of the
    striving rain.
Time I see, and Occasion and Chance in the
    paths and doorways—
Sentinels ready to warn, or soldiers to follow
    the will.
Havilah glows with a yellow gleam in the river
    of Pison.
Steady the horses step, lumber the ponderous
    wains.

The Sleeping City.

The Sleeping City.

I.

THE stars on their little gold threads
   Over the east of the town,
The stars on their little gold threads
  Seem to be hanging down.
Two circles of light are set,
  The moon as cold as a polar steep,
And the yellow disc of the steeple dial
  That wakes in the City of Sleep.

II.

A voice calls in the Night
  To the numberless sleeping souls,
A voice calls in the Night
  When the bell of the steeple tolls :
Bring back, bring back the primal age
  When men could be merry and sing,
Or weep like the young impetuous rain
  That blesses the fields of Spring.

D

III.

The sleepers answer in sleep,
  (They are more than eye can see)
They answer in their sleep :
  Alas it can never be,
For now we are under a spell,
  And the truest tears and the merriest mirth
This many a year, as we know well,
  Have departed from the earth.

IV.

Along the long dark streets
  A spirit sweeps in rapid flight,
Along the long dark streets
  And the pathways of the Night,
And the great roads of the Night,
  And the lamp-rows ranging far,
And the mercy of God is in his heart,
  And on his brow a star.

V.

The clear star sheds its beam,
  Eternal, undefiled,
The clear star sheds its beam
  On many a sleeping child.
In a moment the heavenly light is gone,
  Save from heart, down deep,
And the pallid moon and the yellow dial
  Wake in the City of Sleep.

At the Fair.

At the Fair.

[A PHANTASMAGORY.]

SCENE I.—*The Primal World.   Two Angelic Spirits.*

1ST SPIRIT.

What stir is this ?

2ND SPIRIT.

Huge daughters of the griff
Wrenching at shivering canes.   Below, two beasts,
Uprisen warriors, struggle in the slime,
Churning black ooze with red blood.

1ST SPIRIT.

Horrible !

Pale steam arises from their forest-lair
And dims our great star.   In the firmament
A comet rises.   It is nearly night.

Did God make all these creatures and then set
Them to destroy ?

2ND SPIRIT.

     How shall I speak aright ?
Know this, dear sister—God did make this
  world,
And in the large and ample round of it
Works ever forward ; but works, too, in us,
And shall work in mankind.   If ever blurs
And imperfections cry to thy fair soul
Let their revulsion call to God in thee.
When holy Silence by harsh trumpet-blast
Is shattered, rise to battle for our God.

1ST SPIRIT.

Waft we on further.   In the distance, hark,—
Their roaring's like the sea.   The arid tops
Of hills are soon passed by.   Why look, look
  now,—   [*Pointing to the comet.*
The sullen blaze.

2ND SPIRIT.

     It reaches with large hand
As grasping stars.   Haply it is a sign,
Colossal portent, bending over Earth
Five spreading digits.   [*Exeunt.*

SCENE II.—*The same. Incubi and other evil spirits. A gloomy light.*

1ST VOICE.

Proud with the yellow anointing of Euphrates
What is't you drag ?

2ND VOICE.

Flesh for the altar-fire.

1ST VOICE.

Why, all of you are deckt, and here's a tribe
With pranksome nightshade on their tresses
stuck——

2ND VOICE.

Not stuck.   It grows there freely.

1ST VOICE.

Grows ?

2ND VOICE.

Yes, grows,
As naturally as your horns on you.

[*A loud laugh.*

We've hunted beasts all day.   Come on, old
fellow,
And join our orgie round the fire to-night.

[*Enter* LILITH.

LILITH.

Cease all your noisy folly.   My achievement
Has topped your dullard's conquest over beasts.

INCUBUS (*to a female spirit.*)

Cannot you see the mistress ?   Silence, there,
Or she will score your pretty face for you.

A SINGLE VOICE.

Hail, Lilith !

OMNES.

Lilith, queen and mistress, hail !

LILITH.

Drag that one to the altar who bows not
Before the primal bride.   Now have I wound
Into man's race, as mists of death inlay
With creeping guile the scarpèd mountain-side.
They pass with night, but Lilith charms the
    thought
Of men unto the ending of the world.
I and my serpent Simulation live,
And the great sunlit planet spins its course,
I governing its master.   Man know this,
The vast of nature ?   Little could he know
Of it before, but now—a sort of boar
Whose brain is a most admirable tusk
To rend roots for his gorge : the subtle fool.

Come, all ye spirits, let's see Lilith's trail—
Fetch the Earth Matron with your dizzy spells
And bid her now rend back the clinging folds
That hide futurity.—Sudden and brief.

> [*The spirits, with certain elaborate incantations
> and painful labour, summon the Earth
> Spirit, who appears as a noble matron. The
> storm which had arisen while the spells were
> proceeding at length subsides, but there is
> still only a gloomy light.*

EARTH SPIRIT.

So you compel me hither and I come.
Know this, what is unnatural is brief.
My bosom shall warm many bairns. Of these
A few poor shadows flit before your sense,
And are not. Shall it joy you thus to see
Your marring of my folk ? I tell you this :
Brief is this timeless vision, long the fact,
But everlasting your abhorred fall.

LILITH.

Play not the chorus, dame. We claim the scene.
Burgeon your drowsy capsules, silly seeds,
Flash into red the unripe fruit of Time,—
Let us digest it for ourselves.

EARTH SPIRIT.

See, then.

[*A mist, moving in itself, gathers into dim forms before the trees. These forms slowly become clearer.*

FEMALE SPIRIT.

Larvæ or embryos are these ?

LILITH.

Not so,
But shades of the unfashioned latter world.
You're thinking of the wrong end of the chain.
Be quiet.

[*The inner scene, which is brighter than that in which it is set, represents a fair on the borders of a large town. All sorts of people pass and repass. Shows and booths. A fiend disguised as a Pierrot is talking to a youth.*

PIERROT.

Gay is the place and the summer eve with a
  beautiful devilment is rife.
See the naphtha lamps and the dusty boots of
  the girls—we are just in the height of life.

Youth.

Look at that girl with the beautiful lip, the
  upper lip so tenderly swelling—
Maid for maternity fitted, she, and the strength
  and hope of a children's dwelling.

Pierrot.

Nonsense ! She'll not see thirty again ; but a
  virgin certain, that's just her doom ;
No babes she'll finger, but shams on straw,
  virginity dried in a milliner's room.

Youth.

It's sad. I think such a one should sit on the
  milking stool, or walk in the wealth
Of the infinite odours that waft from meads.

Pierrot.

No doubt it would much improve her health,
But a certain *morbidezza*, you know, is best for
  the waist-tied persons who wait
On the high noblesse ; for when did you see a
  peony on a fashion-plate ?

[A Bishop passes.

Pierrot.

Behold the reverend bishop of souls, and his
  gaiters, truly a quaint device.

YOUTH (*looking at some pictures on a stall*).
My eye was on Judas holding the bag and
  betraying the Son of Man for a price.
[FEMALE SPIRIT.
All this is strange to us.
LILITH.
               But somewhat I
Intuitively rede it.   Certainly
The girls are pretty, and the men—most *wise* !]

HYPNOTIST (*at an open booth*).
Ladies and gentlemen, come here.   I make
By the hypnotic art all people wise,—
Uttering their own thought, not another's.
YOUTH.
                    How
If they have none o' their own ?
HYPNOTIST.
              Why, all have some,
Though some have vastly less than they suppose.
[*A laugh.*
Walk up !   Your crania are transparent !   Hi !
How easily do I out-Röntgen Röntgen !
He shows the bones, but I the very mind.

  [*A crowd gather. Politician sits in chair
    and is hypnotised.*

POLITICIAN.

You've given me a gift.

HYPNOTIST.

What is it, sir?

POLITICIAN.

A ruddy apple.

HYPNOTIST.

And where did it grow?

POLITICIAN.

By the Dead Sea.   O, let me escape from this!
[*A confusion amongst the people.*

HYPNOTIST.

Be quiet, ladies, now do.   For I assure you
That this is strictly scientific.   Hush!

POLITICIAN.

I have done much, and clambered, rung by rung,
Copied and copied, narrowed and refined,
Distinguished, represented, magnified,
Ponderously rolled sonorous monologues,
Then thinned and whittled with a spry grimace,
Word-painting every serviceable lie
To flash on human receptivity.
Thus mouthing have I new-created Nature,
Harnessed her neatly to the party car
And juggernauted the electorates,

Cheered and bribed up to lord it thus, car-high,
Condition——one : that the first brains the
    wheels
Should crush out were—my own. And so aloft,
Mock-humble, crownless, and as if I saw,
Bereft of truth I kinged humanity
And jolted over jubilating fools.

HYPNOTIST.

The gentleman is not well. I will reverse
The passes.   [*He does so.*

POLITICIAN.

Very interesting, that.

What did I say ?

YOKEL.

We could not understand it.

YOUTH.

No wonder. But this mass of unformed speech
May hold some glimpses.   Haply he has lost
In his life-quest of the Expedient, one
Small thing—the eye that can discern the True.

HYPNOTIST (*aside*).

He is a secondary gentleman.
I've seen the world and there are myriads such.
In fact, I think we all are secondary
Since he is. I have phonographed his talk.

YOUTH (*to Pierrot*).

The pretty crowd stare frightened at this show.
What glimpses into depths are in girls' eyes !

PIERROT.

Why, the poor things are mostly shallow.

YOUTH.
Yet
Here methought sudden passed Assyria,
Dark-sweeping, mystic, soon lost in the crowd.
There brownly flashed a barbarous-beauteous
    Hun,
Strength confident, with voluptuous-peeping
    eyes
Flagrantly sweet.   Then in authority
See Mistress Rome with regnant equal mind,—
All girls.   And best of all, here's one, not tall,
But steady in her gait (her footfalls seem,
Like Venus's, her one defect,——— and yet
That realism makes her more ideal,
And the great artist Nature reaches stars
Sic itur—*this* star's pebbles, glebes and seas,
And Momus in the fable was a fool)—
Exalted-lovely, this one, near-removed,
As who should say : " I hold a future world,

Peaceful and wondrous ; but are you the one
Worthy to understand it ?   Heights on heights
I know, and deeps in deeps ; and keep the key
Of a great garden full of sacred flowers
Which only I have lookt at . . . and the sun."
Say, may not such a one for England stand ?
Conscious or not, the strangest potencies
Dwell in these maids.

PIERROT.

    I was young like you once.
Workgirls are these, with cotton shreds on
  skirt ;
In commerce they are just material,
The mechanism and the sexless " hands."
(An aspect full of baseness.   I do not,
Myself, approve of it).   But take it thus :
The lion's look is mock authority,
Most useful in his foraging ; and the girl,
By nature strikes not only with allurement,
But also with respect, to tame brute man,—
Who need not yet be abject for all that.
Just put the eye-trick down at what it's worth—
Nature's stage-property.   It's all illusion.
Talk to the pretty creatures, and you'll see
The canvas and the wood of the *coulisses.*

YOUTH.

Why then am I illusion.   But you're wrong.
I will admit this : Man is beautiful
In his right action, for he's active.   Woman
Is passive—but she's always beautiful.

PIERROT.

Why, your own words recalling, haply I
May teach you wisdom, cynic though I be :
Assyrians, Huns and Romans are they all,
True conquerors *vi et armis;* what you dream,
Of some high blessing or some future world
Of moral power, you'll never find in Woman.
Straighten the Rib, it breaks.   Leave it alone,
(Mahomet says) it's naturally crooked.
I will allow a few distraught exceptions,
Rigidly frigid as a glacial epoch,
(Say, may not such as these for Greenland
      stand ?)
Who give out tracts, are always thirty-three,
And lead the soul to sempiternal gloom.
No.   You will find the intellectual man
To-day upon the rock of Pessimism,
It can't be helped, *mon ami;* so, that cold
And grey inevitable, if you're wise,
You will admit, and seek the wine of life.

I'll tell you what : Trust none of these at all,
I need not say *betray*, for you will find
The pretty gipsies wicked as yourself.
Now, if I were your age, and——   [*Whispers.*

YOUTH.

Pierrot, one thing you cannot gauge : the soul
Of him you chatter to.   What creeds may rise
Or fall, the frame of things is so combined
That even Nature, rising to her height,
Sweeps all your trash away.   There is no thing
Beneath the sky more sacred and more pure
Than the true reverence of the human heart.

PIERROT.

Sounds well, no doubt.   Give me a comic song.
   [*A Ballad Singer, to the accompaniment of a
      banjo, sings to the girls.*

BALLAD.

And it is all for you, dear heart,
   I light the little lamp,
And at the window watch apart
   Above the street all dark and damp.
            For the street is dark and damp
               And the wind is raw and chill,
               But I live to light the little lamp
               And wait your coming still.

In my heart the passion burning
  Will never die away,
On the sill to speak my yearning
  A balsam watches all the day.
        If you should not come by day,
          O then this little light
        Sheds as from my own heart its ray
          To guide you here by night.

Still the meek lamp shall faithful burn,
  And the humble balsam sweet
Await the hour of your return,
  Await the blessing of your feet,
        The blessing of your feet,
          And your gentle, gentle eye,
        Tender as flowers in the wheat
        And pale stars in the sky.

BALLAD SINGER.
Now any of these songs a penny, ladies,
Or three for twopence.

YOUTH.
        Pierrot, see the rogue
Charm pennies from their knotted handker-
    chiefs.
One misery of the modern world is this :

So many patient, sweet Cordelias
Peaked, bound and starved by Gonerils and
     Regans,
So many Cinderellas in the slums.   [*They pass.*

A LORD *and* MILLIONAIRE *enter.*

LORD (*at whom unknown to him the* HYPNOTIST
in the distance is making passes).

So many *feræ naturæ* on my lands,
Landloopers running young and seeming free,
Yet I, to eke my feeble thews and brain,
Have rent, which grasps the instep, drags 'em
     down,
The *bêtes humains.*

MILLIONAIRE.

         Your lordship speaks of lands ;
You'll come on Sunday to my shooting-box ?

LORD.

On Sunday ?   Well, one has to keep the forms.
A man in my position is expected
To set example, and one's private views
Need not be inconveniently displayed.
Our children's wedding is a better time.

DEMAGOGUE (*to a crowd*).

I tell you you're all equal. Stint your work,
Vote for our party. Cry "Down with the
    Lords."

VOICES.

Down with the Lords !

YOUTH (*aside*).

Even so. Opinion, doubly false, divides,
As Sadducees opposed the Pharisees ;
Add both their scantlings, yet the truth is far,
And the age, like a riven boat, sinks down.

PIERROT (*aside*).

Yet his chief meditation was of love,
And he would teach me—teach the Devil him-
    self—
The grounds of virtue, which of course I know,
For every one is just a ground of vice.
This is the great reformer of the age—
(I can't help laughing) and he moons about,
Caught with the sham of bead eyes, and still
    thinking
Of infinite things besides, and doing nought.
And yet he baffles me, for by his brain
He won't subdue the world to his desire.

The momentary emmet stands aloof ;
He has his being outside Time, and so
Ridiculously wastes his time in thinking.
Well,—that's my side, his impotence.   And yet
Of all the futile rascals in the world
None is his fellow.   I am much annoyed.
Give me a good knave or a downright saint,
And I known how to take 'em—if I fail
Or they outrun me—well, the game is played
After the rules, and one may smile and chat ;
But this one does not enter.   O Inertia,
Pyramidal Inertia—there you stand,
Just when the world is humming round about,
    too.

YOUTH.

I catch your words.   The world is humming
    round,
And merrily you think, but not so I.
Choking in lethal shams behold the World,
Whilst cloacas of rhetoric disembogue,
And somewhence rumours come that Heaven
    is not,
And we must decently pretend it is.
Still, still the smirk of the official Christian
Betrays the Best in mankind day by day.

Men sell like sheep, or run about like wolves.
Our priests are lawyers, lawyers the real priests,
The foremost leaders now are the directors,
And now at last the very thought of Man,
His inner Self, is false and secondary.
Some hope from diverse strivings after Truth :
From Cant alone is infinite despair.
That is the sin that cannot be forgiven,
And now we have it; and the world falls down.

[*The crowd thins off. A few children are seen,
skipping.*

CHILDREN.

All in together,
In all sorts of weather,
When the wind blows we all go together.
I saw Pe-ter
Looking out of win-der
Veri-ly, veri-ly
We all fall down.
Windy weather,
Stormy weather,——

[*A distant noise is heard, as of thunder. The
PIERROT is making off.*

YOUTH (*to* PIERROT).

A decent way to bid adieu.

PIERROT.

Adieu ?

'Tis not my word.   In times of public trouble
The wise man simply troubles for himself.
That is the noise of cannon.

[*The booths of the fair are now filled with
    soldiers, and assume the appearance oj
    military tents.   Some mothers run in and
    carry off the children.*

[LILITH (*advancing*).

.   What is this ?

The whole scene changes.   Stay, I bid you
    stay !

THE EARTH SPIRIT.

The phantasms of the future will not speak.
You talk to air.   Yet you dissolve the spell.
More is not given you to know.]

UNWIN BROTHERS, THE GRESHAM PRESS, WOKING AND LONDON.

www.ingramcontent.com/pod-product-compliance
Lightning Source LLC
Chambersburg PA
CBHW020040030726
47499CB00007B/2507